Mynydd Eimon – Private Hell

by

Byron Kalies

Mynydd Eimon – Private Hell
ISBN: 978-1497533455

Late October

Day 1

1 the lady confesses
2 storm warning
3 the thief
4 rage in heaven
5 blonde crazy
6 the set-up
7 the small back room

Day 2

8 out of the past
9 the interrupted journey
10 don't bother to knock
11 open secret
12 angel face
13 angels with dirty faces

Day 3

14 stolen face
15 the killing
16 the thirteenth hour

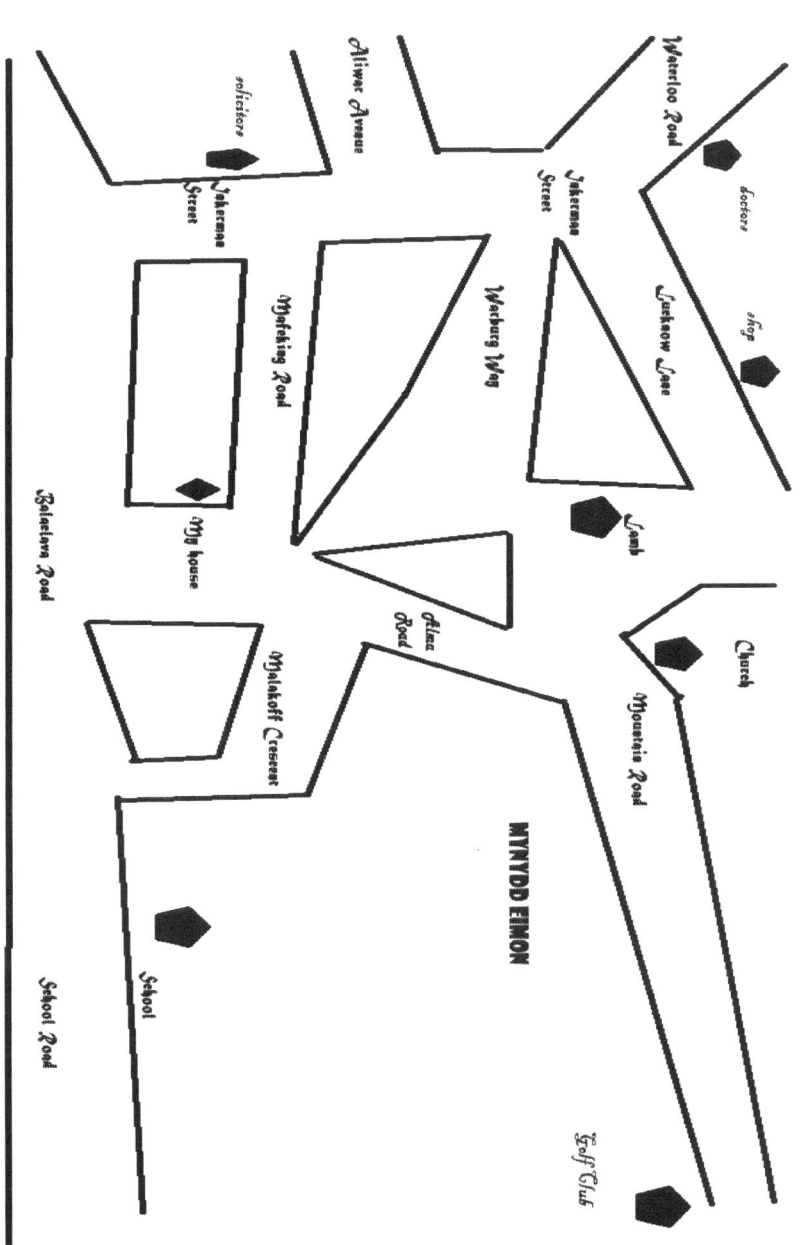

DAY 1

Sky-red – blood red – falling – hit ground hard – not too hard – office - golf club – red carpet – books and books and books - grey safe – easy money – alone – Cai presence outside – falling – vultures – watching – goading – sneering – flying and falling – flying and falling – "destroy the ungodly" - 6 stars – 6 daggers – 1 angel – 3 sticks, vertical like stumps - mother – Mary – stick – gopher wood – battered old goose-necked putter – Bobby – Mary – Molly – Malone – cockles and muscles alive alive-o – her ghost wheels her barrow through the streets – "Sam" – "Wake up " – Run Sam run – "Who built the ark, no-one, no-one. Who built the ark, brother? No-one built the ark"– "Wake up" - Bob – Mary – Sam

1. the lady confesses

It started with a dame. It always started with a dame. Well sometimes it does. This dame was different and unique – like they all were. She was older, a lot older. She was the treasurer, the golf club treasurer. She was respectable, church-going and old. How old? Very old.
It was an ordinary morning, as they all are until something happens. I was walking along grey and grim Malakoff Street and although I didn't know it I was about to be asked to investigate the possible murder of Cai Tywysog.
What was particularly unusual about this possible murder was that I had dreamt that Cai was dead. I had also dreamt that the sky was on fire. I was looking out of the window when I saw someone fall from the roof. It was Cai and his face cracked as he hit the ground. I wasn't sure if the fall had killed him or something had happened before. Neither option mattered too much to him at that particular moment. I also dreamt about an empty safe. Apparently this could signify loss, lack of security or a secret getting out. Or even an empty safe.
Unsurprisingly I felt a little tense this morning.
I knew that Cai wasn't dead as I had seen him just five minutes ago. I had been in the corner shop talking to Mrs Evans' when he had walked in. I picked up my packet of Lucky Strikes and a pint of milk from the counter, gave an assertive nod in Cai's general direction and walked out of the shop. He looked a little pale, but definitely not dead. I walked to the end of Malakoff Street and turned left onto Alma Road.
Alma Road was quiet. Mynydd Eimon was quiet. Not just because it was a Friday morning, but because Mynydd Eimon was quiet. It was boring. It was dull. Mynydd Eimon was a typical Welsh valley village. It looked exactly the same as any other Welsh valley village at any time since the early Victorian Age. It was grey, cold, dull, quiet – calcified in an indeterminate age. It was home. My home.
I walked slowly toward my office. Perhaps office was a little grand in that it was two small rooms on the ground floor of my house. It didn't look much like an office but it was. It was the

office of Sam Watcher, private investigator. That's me. I was a bone fide 'ditectif preifat'. I had a business card and everything. I smiled at the exquisite lettering on the door of the office, "Samael K. Watcher ... Investigations". I didn't have a middle name but thought the K added a touch of class. I went to unlock the door to the outer office, formerly a coalhouse knocked through, but found it had already been opened. I stepped inside and looked at my little universe. The room contained an old black Davenport, two old, old, grey chairs, a bit of carpet and two doors – one to the outside, real world and the other to my inner sanctum. Everything was neat and tidy just as I needed it. There was the light grey carpet and dark grey walls. I had designed the room myself based on films I had seen.

What the room didn't contain was my secretary who I had assumed had unlocked the door. I moved carefully toward my private office and opened the door slowly expecting an intruder. I was correct.

My office and refuge being invaded me nervous. I liked things to be where they should be. My visitor was a dame. She had moved a chair. I looked around to see if anything else had been disturbed. Her coat and bonnet were hanging on the coat stand. I looked around slowly, carefully. I didn't notice anything else. I breathed. The room had a similar colour scheme to the outer office with a larger desk, a fireplace, a Reliable wall safe and a little state of the art, Prestcold fridge, a violated coat stand and a moved chair.

I looked hard at the dame in the chair. She was a frail old woman dressed in a long black dress, grey shawl, and tight bun with a lethal looking hair slide.   From the back she seemed very peaceful as she stared into the empty fireplace. Her coat and bonnet were hanging up on the oak coat stand near the door and she had made herself completely at home. I walked across the room in a business-like manner and placed myself in my chair behind my desk. I turned my chair to face her. I reached in my pocket to get a cigarette, looked at the dame and thought better of it. I picked up a pen from my desk and started twirling it in my fingers.

I breathed. "Aunty Mary." I said a little too loudly, "What are you doing here?"

"It's about a murder, cariad, I'm ashamed to say. It's about the murder of young Cai, my nephew."

"Cai!" I feigned astonishment for some reason, "but I've seen him just now in Mrs Evans'."

She thought for a minute. "Well the murder may not be Cai and anyway it's not today."

"I see." I clearly didn't. I sucked hard on my pen in a way that I thought may convey serious thoughtfulness.

"So what is it you want from me?" I inquired.

"I need some information, some advice if you will."

"Shoot"

"How am I looking if I were to murder someone?" she asked thoughtfully.

I sat down and continued working on my thoughtful expression, "I imagine you would be put in jail Aunty Mary."

"Ah," she paused, "I thought as much. But what about my soul?"

"Well." I paused. "That would be one for you and the priest to negotiate."

She looked disappointed.

"And the soul of the victim?"

"Again your priest would be the one to talk to there."

"Not you?"

"Not me."

"Are you sure about that?"

"Pretty sure."

"And I would definitely go to prison."

I paused to consider the question, "Very, very likely."

She sighed, "So how long would I get?"

"Probably 10 years or life."

We both silently assessed who would win that particular race.

"I'd like you to investigate the murder, when it happens. Would you do that for me?"

I nodded professionally.

"Thank you Samael," she continued as she stood up, "You've been very helpful. Now how much do I owe you?"

"Aunty Mary you know I couldn't take money off you."

"You're a sweet boy." she said as she ruffled my hair and handed me a shilling piece, "Now take it and let's hear no more about it." I took it and helped Aunty Mary put on her ancient grey fur coat and black bonnet. I shivered slightly then I walked Aunty Mary out.

2. storm warning

I came back and sat down behind my desk. I put a cigarette in my mouth and stared at the wall. I'd been away from the village for seven years and nothing seemed to have changed. Aunty Mary looked exactly the same. The streets looked the same. It was grey, dull, depressing, uninspiring. The weather was the same. Always on the verge of raining. Except when it was raining, of course.

You would imagine something would have changed since my childhood. I had. Or at least I thought I had. It was difficult for me to remember. I had what the Cardiff psychiatrist had called 'amnesia' or 'reduplicative paramnesia' or 'just plain old forgetfulness'. I considered it to be not plain, but 'acute' in that I had forgotten the last seven years. On the positive side it didn't look like I had missed much in terms of incident in Mynydd Eimon.

I thought about some of my childhood. Strange and sad though those memories were I remembered quite a lot. I could remember almost all of the past month since I'd returned to Mynydd Eimon. What I wasn't so great on was the bit in between. However, these lost 7 years were beginning to come back. Slowly. Extremely slowly. Not in any particular order. Like mist clearing as you run into it. I could see lights, or patterns or sometimes just feelings. It wasn't as depressing as you'd imagine it would be. It was just what it was. I accepted it. From what I felt I had a lot of shit in my childhood and it didn't bother me too much to not remember all of it for a while. In a way it was like taking a short holiday, well quite a long holiday really. It was difficult to describe. It was difficult to understand. It was difficult to be me.

I squashed the cigarette in a glass tray and focused. Something was wrong. Something about Aunty Mary's manner had alerted my senses. I had read somewhere that a private eye should always trust his instincts. My senses were tingling as I replayed the scene in my head, word by word. I couldn't help but notice how unsure she was of who she would kill, or when. I wondered why she had decided to visit me. I would be of no use to her. She must have known. She knew all the answers I had given her. She knew the odds of her, or anyone, in Mynydd Eimon going to prison for murder, or anything were astronomical. I'm pretty sure there was a police force in the welsh valleys somewhere but I can't remembering ever seeing a police officer in real life. And, most remarkably of all, Aunty Mary hadn't once mentioned golf. It might be an idea to take a look at the golf club.

I wondered why she wore her Sunday best to visit. And that bonnet. What was it about the bonnet? And how old was she? She had always seemed ancient and on the verge of death. Something clearly wasn't quite right. I remember her from when I was a child and she looked after me. Before that even I remembered that she had frightened me looking at me in my pram. People say you don't remember those things. I remembered that. I remember that when she leaned in and looked at me in my pram she wore the same bonnet that she wore today. I shuddered.

Aunty Mary's life was the golf club. She was the cleaner, finance organiser, minute taker, and book keeper. Her official title was Women's captain although I never saw her play golf and never saw another lady member she could captain. The golf club was Aunty Mary's life. Yet she hadn't mentioned it once. What was really going on at the golf club?

As a poor boy from the bottom end of the village, golf had been as alien to me as English people for the first 10 years of my life. The only people I knew who played golf were priests, headmasters or solicitors. I had always thought it was not the game for me, or any proper Welshman.

I lit another cigarette from the butt of the previous one – a terrible habit I know. I reflected on the time I'd been back in the village and set up my detective agency. My agency was surprisingly busy for a small village at the north end of the South Wales valleys. I had dealt with a number of cases, all unexciting. However they all paid the rent. In fact the investigating business was remarkably, consistently, metronomically, suspiciously steady.

I heard my secretary making secretary-type noises in the outer office and I reached out to press the intercom to check my appointments. I then realised I wasn't a proper American private detective who could afford a proper intercom. I had planned on getting a proper intercom but hadn't quite got around to it. I would some time, I mused. I looked at my finger hovering over my writing pad and felt pleased no-one had seen me. I wondered where I had got the idea for an intercom. I thought really hard. I remembered films, of private eyes, Bogart, Bacall. But where had I seen the films? I remember watching them with my father, sister. Somewhere. Sometime.

I looked at my framed, signed print of Bobby Jones on the wall and thought about my own short golfing career. Why had I loved golf? Again the image of my father leapt into my mind. Perhaps it was really time to take a closer look at the golf club? And what was Aunty Mary's problem with me and the priest? She talked about her soul. Maybe I needed to take a closer look at the priest as well? Perhaps it was time to take a closer look at a lot of things? Maybe I was overthinking everything? Maybe not?

I emptied the ash tray into the bin. I took the bin and emptied it into the bigger bin outside. I washed my hands carefully, thinking. I picked up my hat, I did have a proper hat, and walked out of the door without telling anyone where I was going - not that I had anyone else to tell – parents lost, no wife, girlfriend or children to worry about me. I looked around. Even my secretary seemed to have disappeared again. The only things I had were a coat, a hat and a gun. Well, I did have a house and a business. So, perhaps I had quite a few things.

I walked toward the door thinking, yeah, perhaps it was time to take a closer look at a lot of things? The golf club. The priest. My life. Perhaps it was time to look at a lot of things? Well no. Probably the golf club and the priest would be enough to be going on with. I finally stepped out of my office with a headache but a happy thought; I had a proper paying client and could officially start investigating. It was a job, not a hobby I kept reminding myself.

3. the thief

I locked the office door behind me. There were mythological villages in Wales where there is an inbuilt trust and community spirit. We are a giving, trusting and caring people, apparently. I didn't seem to have been blessed with that particular Welsh gene. I locked the door and then rattled the handle to make sure it was properly locked.
I walked distractedly north along Alma Road. The houses were all the same – terraced, grey, cramped, old, cold, functional, miner-built, not cute not cute at all. I turned into Waterloo Road. I passed the 'Square' that was more of an isosceles triangle than anything. I saw that there was a light on in the church, thought about going in, didn't, and continued. I turned onto the mountain road, called Mountain Road, toward the golf club. This was the final road of Mynydd Eimon. I felt sick.
Mynydd Eimon was a small, squeezed village where the road stopped because it crashed into the mountain. There was no passing traffic through Mynydd Eimon. It was a dead end village, back end. If you were in Mynydd Eimon you were in it for a reason. The only viable reason was that you lived here. I looked up at the sky. It was, unsurprisingly, grey. I could feel the cold of the gun in my pocket as I checked that the safety catch was on. I had never used it once in the 31 days I had had it and didn't intend to use it. But these were tense times and you could never tell what was around the corner.
It was a steep climb to the golf club and as I reached the top of the track I could see the white snow across the black mountains in the distance and a smattering of red and yellow flags positioned along the horizon. It was cold, very cold. The sign said 'Visitors Welcome' – this wasn't true. There were few visitors, they were never welcomed and they never returned. Somehow the club survived on its handful of members and the occasional inbred social function in the Clubhouse.
Yet there never seemed to be any panic about finance. I had been a member since I was 11 years old yet had never received a request for golf fees. I attributed this to the attitude of the treasurer and the incompetence of the secretary and committee.

The clubhouse was a functional, squat, grim building. The kindest way to describe it was - unremarkable. As I approached the clubhouse from the half- finished, pothole riddled road I could see Amos Caddoc, village doctor, closest to me, with his head down. He was 50 yards away, seated at the table studying his cards with some of the other committee members. I moved out of sight, behind the row of misshapen trees along the drive. As I moved my head around the tree I could see my uncle on Caddoc's left. The head honcho himself. El presidente. Mister. Daniel. Llewellyn. The boss. The main man. Y dynio. Solicitor. Entrepreneur. All round good egg. For some instinctive Pavlovian reason I gripped the handle of my gun and squeezed it. I relaxed. Breathed and lit a cigarette and decided to carry on playing the game. I smoked for a while as I pretended to hide behind the trees and they pretended not to notice. Or perhaps I was being paranoid. Llewellyn and his cronies looked like a family of jackals crouched over a carcass as they stooped over the card table. Slamming cards down and squawking intermingled. There was much deep concentration interspersed with cackles of laughter and banging the table as they fought over the folded notes in the pot.

None of them looked up as I slid around the side of the club house, opened the door and entered the building. The corridor was decorated with expensive wallpaper and a plush burgundy carpet that totally deadened my footsteps. I hadn't been here for many years but still recognised the trophy cabinet with an array of silver cups and plates inscribed with names of past champions. Pride of place, of course, was the Ystrad Cup with the name Cai Tywysog all over it. I was suddenly overcome with a strong feeling. It's wasn't hate, as such. More of jealousy. I had always wanted to win this trophy but never had.

On the wall next to the cabinet I saw a new treasure. It was a battered old goose-necked putter in a glass case. I recognised it from somewhere. From every dream I've had in the past few months. I saw the title underneath -"Calamity Jane – presented to Mynydd Eimon Golf Club by S.L. Watcher".

I knocked softly on the door of the secretary's office. I counted to ten waiting for no-one to reply then gently opened the door.

The secretary was a headmaster and tended to work on a Friday so I had felt reasonably confident as I entered the room. The safe was where I had dreamt it was last night, hidden behind the writing table. The whole scene was as I had dreamt it. I had had a lot of dreams in the time I had returned to the village. They weren't all as specific as this one though. It was then that I heard a scream from outside. I ran to the door and couldn't help noticing that the sky was on fire. I saw someone fall from the roof. It was Cai and his face cracked as he hit the ground. But that was from this morning's dream. I didn't really happen – I told myself.

I lit a cigarette to clear my head, took the key I had lifted from Aunty Mary's coat pocket out of my own pocket and opened the very old-fashioned safe. The door of the safe looked old and very solid. It opened easily, smoothly and deathly quietly though. Someone had obviously looked after this carefully. I noticed that the hinges had recently been oiled and cleaned. Almost as if someone had wanted the safe to open quietly.

There was a lot of money in a range of differing denominations in the safe, a number of forms, a gun and an old book that looked as if it should have had a sticker on it saying "Old folder with lots of interesting information in it". It was black, ancient and had three large, thick, old-fashioned elastic bands around it holding loose papers and photographs. The cover had a label that said 'ACCOUNTS BOOK' – which it clearly wasn't. I took off the elastic bands and flicked quickly through the book at diary entries, old photographs, newspaper cuttings, pieces of ancient parchment, Latin verses and what looked like recipes. I re-tied the elastic bands around the folder and put it under my coat.

As I walked back down the hill toward the village I reflected on the morning. I had the feeling I was being manipulated. I didn't particularly mind this as it was becoming quite interesting, and on a Friday there wasn't a lot to do in Mynydd Eimon. I decided I'd go with the flow for the moment and take a closer look at the folder. I'd also take a closer look at the priest. Perhaps it was time …. Enough of that the headache was coming back.

The steep and winding road led to the church at the bottom of Mountain Road. I toyed with the idea of taking the package to my office, but decided to hide the package where I used to hide other things when I was a child – under the hedge that surrounded the church. I took a deep breath and prepared to visit Father Barry.

4. rage in heaven

I approached the church – functional, angular, grey, holy, grim, and foreboding - with a degree of foreboding. I saw an owl perched on the roof. Not a good sign. I'd been told that I used to be a regular church-goer as a child – choir, rugby team, trips to the seaside at Easter. However I had no memory of this part of my life and couldn't fill in any blanks as a stood in front of the huge arched door.
I could hear an angry voice from inside the church. A familiar, angry voice, from another of my dreams or memories. A recurring dream or recurring memory. I stopped dead and listened.
"And all shall be smitten with fear
And the Watchers shall quake,
And great fear and trembling shall seize them unto the ends of the earth.
And behold! He cometh with ten thousands of His holy ones
To execute judgement upon all,
And to destroy all the ungodly:
And for all of you sinners there shall be no salvation,
But on you all shall abide a curse.
And you will know my name is the Lord when I lay my vengeance upon you!"
The last line was screamed into my face as the door opened and the priest stared at me. His breath smelled of whisky. My olfactory cortex remembered this from somewhere. The priest was still Father Barry. He knew me from my childhood – even though I didn't.
 "Uplifting sermon father", I commented, "Not talking about me were you?"
"Are you a sinner Samael", he smiled.
I shrugged
"Samael, Samael, Samael" he muttered.
"Father, Father, Father" I couldn't stopped myself replying.
Father Barry was old – very old. He looked like a very tall praying mantis. He was dressed in all white and had the three day stubble of a tramp, or a tall stubbly praying mantis. With him

the tramp look seemed the best bet. He smelt of whisky, incense and the bible.

On the positive side something was beginning to stir in my memory. I remembered that I detested this man. I couldn't remember exactly why but that didn't seem to matter too much – I knew I hated him. When he spoke again I remembered that I hated his voice. He had the whiniest voice. I was not a fan.

"What are you looking for Samael?" he wheezed as he led me gently up the aisle.

"In general?" I replied watching my feet to ensure I didn't fall into his trap of mirroring his steps as we walked.

"No. In particular."

I stopped. "You father. I'm looking for you." I lied

He stopped and looked at me for a good few seconds. Then he started walking again. "Why are you lying to me Samael?" he smiled. "I'm a priest and I know everything. I can always tell when you're lying. I always could. You have a 'tell'?"

"Really" I replied, almost feigning interest walking with him. There was something about Father Barry that made me want to slap him.

"Yes. I can tell when you lie because your lips move."

I stopped.

"Hilarious." I announced.

I asked a question that had been troubling me;

"How old am I Barry?"

"Father Barry"

"How old am I Father Barry?"

"Don't you know?"

"You know I don't?"

"*The glory of young men is their strength, but the splendour of old men is their grey hair.*"

I looked at him. I realised I wasn't going to get a lot of sense with direct questions.

"Tell me about Mary, Barry. Tell me about Mary."

"A troubled soul."

"Really – how so?"

"She's never really been one of us."

"Us?"

"How could she," he mused. He feigned thinking, pretending that this little speech wasn't prepared, "She's a servant, not a martyr, a watcher not a witness. "

I must have looked especially confused. He tried to clarify.

"One of us." He repeated louder.

I tried another tack, "She wants you to look after her soul."

He laughed, "Me?"

"She says she may kill someone?"

"Cai?"

"You know?" I continued, "Do you think she will?"

He thought animatedly, "Possibly. Possibly."

"Why?"

"Because he's not really one of us."

"Isn't he?" I was astonished – genuinely.

"Well" he backtracked, "yes but no"

He clarified, "He is but he isn't. He was but he isn't."

I had had enough of this particular line of questioning. I had the sense that Father Barry was working to some kind of a tight script. Tight and shallow. Perhaps I could find some more general information.

"Why are we so special, Father Barry?" I fished.

"Because we have certain powers, of course"

"Such as?"

"We can mess with time a little."

"Really?"

He continued, "How old are you?"

"Well I was born in 1909 and I was 14 when I left. Apparently I left for 7 years so…"

"Oh Samael, Samael, Samael. What year do you think it is?"

I had some ideas; 1930, 1940, 1950 or something in between. I must have looked confused.

"It's just a number Sam. You have your head full of books, films from the 1940s. Doesn't that seem strange?"

It didn't. I realised I was being manipulated and drawn away from my purpose.

"Tell me about my mother, Father Barry?"

"Ah!" he pressed his fingers together and asked, "Why now?"

"I was told never to answer a question with a question, weren't you?"
"I was, but why now?"
"It's time."
"It's time" he reflected, and sighed. "I suppose you're right - it is time.
Tell me Samael what do you remember of her?"
"There you go again. I remember nothing. You know this."
"She disappeared around the same time as you did. Just left one winter evening and left you and your sister alone in the house. She has never returned."
"Or her body has never been found", I interjected with a theory of my own.
"Yes. It's a mystery."
"Father – this I know. What was she like?"
"She was perfect."
This came as something of a shock to me as I'd never heard anything of her character. The few people I'd tried to talk to in my 31 days back had faked sympathy and then quickly changed the subject.
"Perhaps too perfect" he continued enigmatically.
"No-one is too perfect."
"Perhaps you're right." he agreed.
This was getting nowhere.
"And you father…what's your story?"
"You still ask lots of questions Samael, don't you?"
"Still?"
"Yes. You were always in trouble for asking lots of questions. Too many questions"
I had had enough of this enigmatic nonsense. I stopped, looked at the altar, drifted away and recalled a lesson from my schooldays, 'altar, place of slaughter or sacrifice'. I could hear the teacher reciting. Barry's voice awoke me.
"I'm a priest Samael. I know everything."
"Do you know where all the bodies are buried Father?"
He smiled.
"Most of them." He admitted, "Most of them."

Father Barry walked into his sacristy and closed the door notifying that our time was up. I walked back through the church whistling for no reason I could think of. Perhaps it was to show I wasn't as afraid as I thought I was. It didn't work.

I wandered around the narthex looking for something, anything. It seemed unusual that Father Barry had disappeared leaving me alone. It's almost as if he wanted me to find something. Inside a small cupboard behind a curtain I accidentally came across a plain sheet of paper. I l looked around before I lit a cigarette, inhaled deeply and read. It was a funeral service. There was no indication of whose funeral it was. Looking at the service I realised Father Barry had chosen a reading. It was a reading I had heard many times before as a young boy. We had it drilled into us at Sunday school by father Barry and Auntie Mary. It was the story of the Good Watchers and the Bad Angels from The Book of Jubilees. There didn't seem to be many laughs in it agreed but why use it for a funeral service though? I read;

> "*And every one sold himself to work iniquity and to shed much blood, and the earth was filled with iniquity. And after this they sinned against the beasts and birds, and all that moves and walks on the earth: and much blood was shed on the earth, and every imagination and desire of men imagined vanity and evil continually.*"

I crushed my cigarette of the wall and left feeling I was being played for a sucker. The church. The office. It was all too easy.

"*As flies to wanton boys are we to the gods.*" I remembered.

Still. I was bored. What else was there to do in Mynydd Eimon on a Friday?

I picked up my package from under the hedge and walked back to my office. I was shivering. I needed a drink.

5. blonde crazy

10 minutes later I was sitting safely behind my big desk in my private office. I was thinking. I had locked the folder in my drawer for the moment. I had been tempted to look at it but decided not too. I knew myself too well. If I had started I would need to look at everything, thoroughly, in great detail. It wasn't the time now. I had people to see, places to go. Who and where wasn't quite clear yet, but it soon would be. I had a pen in my hand and I was drawing concentric circles on the newly polished surface of my mahogany desk. Boy, was I going to be in trouble. I stopped doodling at the thought.

From the outer office I heard a woman scream and a chair tip over. I continued expanding my double spirals with increased concentration. I added fire, birds, skulls and the moon. I was my psychologist's dream. The screams continued and it sounded as if someone had been pushed to the floor. I heard my secretary swearing.

As slowly as any gumshoe had ever move I stood up and walked to the door. I opened it to see a raven haired woman and a blonde locked in a wrestling match. My secretary, Lily, was the brunette.

 Lily was my ideal worker. She didn't cost me a cent. She was perfect. Physically she was pretty, well rounded and strong. She was mentally extremely strong, or incredibly stubborn (take your pick), as well. When she had turned up to apply for the job I hadn't yet advertised we haggled about money in a curious way. I tried to offer her a little money, payable later when we were busy. She insisted on getting paid nothing. She won the argument. She was a brilliant secretary, ruthlessly efficient, obedient and very, very protective. She was however, utterly humourless. She was also not blessed, or burdened with any shades of grey. She did what was asked – no less. Waiting for Lily to surprise you was as futile as waiting for a good simile to end this description.

I knew very little about her except she had known my mother but wouldn't talk to me about her. Mother apart though she was my main source of information. She seemed to know everything about me. She was my rock. I knew very little about her life though. I guess someone was paying her, possibly a relative of mine – like most Welsh villages it seemed that practically everyone was a cousin. Or perhaps she was working for free out of the kindness of her heart. Either way it had the same financial outcome for me.

My thoughts drifted. I was suddenly brought back to earth by the sound of a strangled cry. Lily appeared to have the upper hand at the moment. She had the blonde in a half nelson with a firm, strangle hold. It was a nice move and one the blonde seemed incapable of countering. Lily looked at me. I tried to look annoyed.

"Lily. Is this how we treat clients?" I asked in my sternest voice.

"You told me you didn't want any visitors. She wouldn't take no for an answer."

The blonde croaked, "I have to talk to you. It's important."

The blonde was no match for Lily. She was a bantamweight at best grappling with a middleweight. Her dress was getting creased and dirty as she looked up at me. She looked tired and very familiar.

"I'm busy." I said and turned, wanting to get back to my office and my doodling.

"We need to talk. It's important"

"Go away." I started to move toward the sanctity of my office.

"It's about your parents." she continued.

I turned toward her. I didn't need this right now.

"I told you I'm busy. I don't need this now sis."

"But Sam I've remembered something."

I shrugged,"5 minutes sis."

I looked back at Lily and nodded. Lily released her even more reluctantly than I'd opened the door 30 seconds ago.

I took in the skinny, pretty, angry blonde as she stood up and brushed down her dress. She looked like trouble I didn't need. Lily scowled. I mouthed 'sorry' and the blonde walked ahead of me into my room. She sat in my chair. She looked at my half-completed doodle on the desk and smiled.

I had been back in the village 31 days now and my sister hadn't been very forthcoming about my life. When I'd asked her questions every one of those 31 days she'd said in 31 different ways that she could only remember the same as I could. I was starting to think that I believed her.

I had sort of faded back into this Mynydd Eimon life like a confused, Welsh ghost. It wasn't like 1 minute I was asleep, the next I was wide awake. It was more like one minute I was asleep, the next I was a little awake. Then I was more awake. Then I was walking along the street thinking about how I was figuring out if I were asleep or not. The past month had been like a dream or a part of a dream. I was tired though. Really tired.

It was only now that I could remember with absolute clarity what had happened the previous day. It was finally total recall; day 1.

"Drink?" I asked as I walked to the small fridge.

"You know I do." she replied.

I smiled gently and mixed some cocktails. I poured them into glasses, added ice and sat opposite my sister.

I handed her a glass, lifted mine up, smiled sideways and said, "Here's looking at you kid."

She smiled gently as well and started talking. 10 minutes later she had gone and left me with an empty glass and another headache.

I thought for a long while after my sister left. Then I looked at my watch, stood up quickly and reached for my coat. As it pulled on my hat I remembered the folder from the golf club and decided I'd better keep it out of harm's way. I opened the desk drawer, took it out, put it in the wall safe and locked it. As I walked through the outer office I tossed the key at Lily;

"Guard that with your life Lily"

I was confident it would be safer with Lily than a Godfather's grandmother.

"Where are you going?" she asked.

"Out" I answered and opened the door to the street.

"Where", came the voice from behind me.

"Back to school" I replied and walked out.

6 the set up

It had started to snow – grey, grey snow that drifted down from a grey, grey sky. I began to get upset about that until I realised I couldn't really do anything about it and I needed to keep all my anger for the school.

I turned right out of my office then left onto Balaclava Road towards my old school. As I approached School Lane I could hear the screams of the handful of children. I was surprised there were so few children as I saw them racing toward me and away from the school. In true Victorian fashion the school resembled a Dickensian fortress. The building was pushed back against the mountain and the only way in or out was one narrow lane. The only way to attack it would be head on. I reached the school gates, crossed the playground, opened the heavy wooden door and walked along the echoing corridor. I moved along the familiar corridor resplendent with poems, paintings, silver paper and coloured paper. I found some of my own – still looking pristine, untarnished with age. A composition entitled 'What I want to be when I grow up' – By Sam Watcher aged 9 and ¾. It had a drawing of a private eye dressed remarkably as I was currently dressed. I looked at the neat handwriting. I was pleased with myself.

I peered into the 7 empty, messy classrooms with the dank smell of caged children still clinging to the walls.

The Headmaster's room was protected by the School Secretary's office "Miss K. Rees, School Secretary" and the door was open. As I approached I looked through the small, glass windows and saw Miss Rees. She was being extremely busy doing school secretary things. I crouched down for no good reason and scooted past the doorway. I pulled myself up straight, adjusted my tie as I arrived outside the solid ash door that announced "Mr P. Penn - Headmaster". I sat on an old, dark, well-worn chair outside the room – a place I remembered fearing for a large portion of my school life. The school was one of the places I had the clearest of memories. Not of specific events – just feelings. I instinctively

feared this purgatorial chair. Not that I remember actually sitting on this chair often. I had the feeling I was good.
I breathed deeply and knocked on the door. Miss Rees apparated behind me. Miss Rees was the embodiment of a shrew - small with a long, twitching nose, nearly invisible eyes, nimble, silent, grey, woollen coat, pair of glands on the flanks and rump which secrete a strong odour and a long, graceful tail. Well, perhaps not the tail.
"Watcher. What have you been up to now?"
I looked at the floor and mumbled "Nothing miss". Then remembered I was grown up and tried to smile and pretend I was joking.
She looked at me unconvinced. "Mr Penn is busy and doesn't want to be disturbed."
Mr Penn opened the door and beckoned me in with a kindly smile.
"Thank you Miss Rees. Watcher we need to talk. It's important. Come in."
I adjusted my face to give the expression of someone who had won a small victory but didn't want to gloat too much about it. However when I turned around Miss Rees had gone and I could hear her in her office carrying out more noisy school secretarial tasks.
I entered the room. It was exactly the same as I remembered it from my dreams and bits of my memory. I looked around and there were books everywhere. There was a shelf of old, grey Welsh text books above Mr Penn's head with a folder next to it. There were English and Welsh text books scattered around the room. The three canes were in the corner standing upright next to each other like precarious cricket stumps. The room was musty, dark, Welsh and cluttered, rather like the mind of its tenant.
"I hear you're taking up the great game of golf again Samael?"
"Am I?" I replied.
Penn looked like what he was – a sad, slightly disturbed, cartoon Welsh head teacher. He was the Welshest Welshman I had ever known. I had no idea where he came from but I'd guess it could

be measured and found to be the epicentre of Wales. He was short, dark and gruff. He loved the sound of his own voice, which was just as well as, from memory, no-one else did. He was also a human thesaurian avalanche. Additionally, his sentences were so, so, so slow and drawn out. He could make an excited Oscar winner's speech sound like a very, very long reading from the Mabinogion. He was also the most impatient man I had ever met. It was like sitting on a volcano. A Welsh volcano, llosgfynydd Cymraeg,
"You used to be really, really good. Tremendous potential" he said this in a very Welsh way emphasising the 'Tre'. ,
"Tremendous potential" he repeated.
"Sit, sit."
I sat, sat.
"So, what was I like as a child?" I asked. I had to bite my tongue not to add "sir".
"You always wanted to be in the movies, or a detective. " He stopped to look at me carefully. He started again, "Even better you wanted to be a detective in the movies." He stopped. He started again, "Yes, a detective. What happened to that?"
I looked at him with 'hilarious' in my eyes.
He laughed and shook as if it were the funniest thing in the world. It wasn't.
"So young Samael. You're still asking lots of questions are you?" he droned.
"I'm trying, but I'm not getting lots of answers."
He stopped to think, then continued, "So, Samael, tell me. "He paused, "What is it that you want to know?"
"My sister says I tried to kill myself when I was fourteen. Why would I do that?"
"Why would anyone do that?" he asked redundantly.
"Why did I do that?" I insisted.
The headmaster slowly adopted the sitting praying mantis position with his hands folded in prayer and his chin resting on them.
"You were unhappy" he eventually announced.
"I sort of worked that out, sir."
"You got in with a bad crowd."

"Where?"
"At the golf club"
I didn't say anything.
He followed up with, "Vernal Section".
I didn't say anything.
"Youth, glaslanc, adulescentia, junior" he translated.
He closed his eyes and continued, "When I was a windy boy and a bit and the black spit of the chapel fold."
"Why is golf so important in Mynydd Eimon?"
"Golf is perfect – par, one under, handicaps. It's all maths. Numbers – 6, 13, 17, 18. "
I didn't say anything.
"Maths is the devil in detail."
I didn't say anything again.
"As Saint Augustine said, *'the good Christian should beware of mathematicians. Mathematicians have made a covenant with the devil to darken the spirit and to confine man in the bonds of Hell.'*"
I continued not to say anything.
Penn continued "We love golf – it's beautiful – pure - perfect. "
I didn't say anything, yet again and pretended to look bored.
He opened his eyes, stopped and I saw an instant of panic in his eyes as he replayed the past 30 seconds wondering if he had said too much. He concluded that he hadn't, but realised he was close to actually saying something useful so he stopped. I'd worked all this out in point 6 of a second, of course. I could have been wrong, but in my business you learn to trust your instincts. I knew I had the measure of Mr Penn so I relaxed and waited for my opportunity.
We stared at each other looking for weaknesses.
He settled back and thought deeply. He weighed up a number of factors – what he could say, what he couldn't, how much to lie, how much truth to tell. He made his decision, chose his script and delivered his homily;
"Up until the time you were thirteen you were the perfect child"
"Perfect?" I interjected.
He paid no heed, he was off and the next few minutes were his carefully worded, carefully thought out sermon. I got the feeling he was reading out this sermon from a prompt somewhere

behind me. He wasn't – I looked around at the shelves behind me. But it definitely felt like it.

"You were a lovely child – bright, inquisitive, a bit cheeky but plenty of charm. Enough charm to get away with it………. before you were thirteen. Then you became a loner, a recluse, an outsider if you will. You went off the rails."

Mr Penn had this wonderful Welsh way of making everything sound like a very interesting shopping list. All style. No substance.

"You were still a remarkable golfer. A quite remarkable golfer but a charmless person on the golf course. You played and beat practically all the golfers in that year. Everyone except Cai. He was the professional so no-one beat him. You remember? No, of course you don't. But you were extraordinary."

I pretended to look bored. But carefully choose my tactic.

"Did I beat you?" I interrupted

He switched out of his scripted revere. I felt his patience was starting to wane with me.

"Did I?" I repeated

"No."

"No?" I goaded him.

"I never played you."

"Why not?"

He tried to return to the script.

"You were the youngest winner of the junior medal at 13, junior captain at 13, winner of the senior Champion Putter at 13…"

"13 seems to be coming up a lot."

"I'm trying to tell you something," he practically screamed at me.

"How old am I, sir?"

He stood up shaking, "Fuck you."

I started to cry.

"No-one could ever help you could they. Enough now – off you go I've things to do."

He walked out leaving me to pretend to dry my eyes on my handkerchief. Penn had always been a sucker for the tears.

I waited a few seconds then picked up my school record from the shelf behind me. I hid it under my coat.

He knew I was coming to see him somehow. That took some doing. I hadn't decided myself until I'd finished talking with my sister. That was interesting. Who was pulling the strings? I could guess but I wasn't a good guesser.

I left the school without seeing Mr Penn or Miss Rees again. What game were we playing? I wondered, and am I winning? I doubted it. I doubted it very much.

How had he known I was going to visit him? I had only decided myself a few minutes before I left the office. Why had I lied about what my sister had told me? And why did he act as if it was true? Was it true? And how old was Penn? He looked younger now than I remembered him from my school days.

7. the small back room

The Lamb was busy. People were talking, happy, being noisy, being annoying. The pub was sepia-toned. The staff were professionally friendly. In one corner there was an intense game of crib and don. The other corner had a game of devil amongst the tailors. These were the highlights of the entertainment scene in Mynydd Eimon. This was entertainment in its loosest, most pathetic sense.
I looked around but even with my eyes shut and even with *my* memory I could tell where everyone would be sitting. It's called a result of my dissociative amnesia, I think. It's like remembering the world as a 4 dimensional jigsaw with the 4th dimension have half the pieces missing.
There hadn't been a new face in the pub for as long as I could remember. The only progression had been boys turning 15 and paying someone to buy their first timid, illegal, drinks in the back bar egged on by their experienced, 16 year old friends. At 16 they would progress to their first communion at the bar. What a day that was for the parents and congregation. The invited guests, new suits, gifts, Father Barry saying a few words before serving the victim with Guinness and crisps. I'm joking. It wasn't always like that. Or rather it hadn't been like that for a while. I noticed now how few children there were. My return must have taken the average age of the pub congregation to below 3 score and 10 for the first time in 3 pair and 1 years. However old I was.
I sat with my back to the wall, facing the door that led to the small dark room. I had read somewhere that this is what private eyes did, or was that secret agents, or gunmen? Whoever invented the process seemed to have hit on a great idea. I sat and waited. This, waiting, wasn't something I did well. Which was curious in a way as one of the few skills required for a good private detective was patience. Still, who said I was any good. I was waiting for the meeting in the back room to finish. This was a Friday and every Friday there was a meeting of the 'Friends of Mynydd Eimon'. No-one was really sure what the 'Friends of Mynydd Eimon' did. It was assumed they were a hard working charitable organisation with the sole purpose of helping the

community of Mynydd Eimon. However, they never organised charitable events, never held raffles, dances, coffee mornings, bingo or whist drives. They did seem to meet regularly though. I had been in the pub when they arrived; priest, headmaster, doctor, solicitor, golf club lackeys all and Aunty Mary. I had talked briefly to Aunty Mary earlier and managed to slip the safe key back into her pocket. Then I sat and waited. I didn't know what I was waiting for, but I had the feeling something was brewing. I could hear noise from the small room, heated arguments and the occasional squeak, screech, scream, howl, bleat and hom hom. I would have tried to get closer but noticed the twins, Dai Proper and Dai Copy at the door, not exactly keeping guard but not exactly leaving the doorway clear for people to pass either. It was a very contrived chat they were having and they stared at me a great many times like they were livestock guardian dogs such as a Carpathian Shepherd Dog displaying the key qualities of trustworthiness, attentiveness and protectiveness, with the added bonus of implied violence. Cai arrived, saw me, ordered a pint for himself and a bourbon for me. Now I could confirm that he still wasn't dead. He looked alive. He looked exactly like a golf pro should look – blonde, tanned (amazingly as he had lived all his life in a small, dark, valley in Wales), tall and athletic. Healthy. He looked annoyingly healthy and very much alive.
"You're not dead." I confirmed as he sat down.
"No. Not yet." he joked.
I hadn't talked at any length to Cai for a long time. I couldn't remember ever doing it actually. He had been a few years older than me. We had become my best friend when I was around 13. We'd been inseparable for a year. We used to go everywhere together, sharing everything, apparently.
"I hear you've been busy" he remarked sipping at his drink.
"Just being nosey" I replied.
"And..."
"And I don't think I found out anything."
"What do you want to know?" he asked
"Everything. Tell me about me."

In the next 15 minutes Cai told me everything he wanted to tell me about me. How I was a smashing friend, bit of a loner, terrific at golf, got in with a bad lot, Vernal Section, went off the rails a little, mother ran away from home and I had some sort of a breakdown, went away and returned a few months ago, blah, blah, blah.
"Where did I go?" I asked
"Away."
"Away where?" I asked politely
"Abroad I think"
"England?"
"No, proper abroad – America."
"Doesn't anyone know exactly where I went?"
"The doctor I expect." He nodded toward my sister. She was on a different table.
"I see". I didn't.
I casually brought up the subject of Cai's father.
"What happened to your father Cai?"
"What do you mean?"
"Well – did he die? Go abroad?"
"I really don't know and I'm not sure I want to talk about it." He had a prim, upper-class, clipped way of speaking. Which again was strange considering he had apparently lived his entire life in Wales.
I nodded.
"So what do you remember about him?" I continued
"Nothing really. I never saw him. Or my mother. I was raised by Aunty Mary. I asked, of course but no-one would ever tell me. There were rumours, teasings in school about him being dead. Killed by your father even. Stabbed apparently. But I didn't believe it. I just don't know."
"Did it upset you?" I asked.
"Not really. I remember going home in tears to Aunty Mary and she told me not to be so ridiculous. She made a joke and said Uncle Sam would never use his hand, he'd use a gun – it would be easier. It made me laugh."
I looked at Cai carefully. He was laughing. Weird.

"So you really don't remember me at all? Not even when we were in school together?" Cai asked somewhat sorrowfully.
"Nope. Nothing" I lied.
I remember he was really, really good at golf. He always used to beat me. I hated that. I did remember something, but not about school. I knew vividly that I disliked Cai immensely. I'm not sure exactly why but I knew he had hurt me some time in the past. Not in any emotional, namby pamby sense but in a painful, cruel torturing way. I didn't know how, when or where but apart from those minor details I knew it with deep, total certainty. I hated him for it. Something bad had happened to me and I knew Cai was involved.
"Same again?" I asked cheerfully as I got up and went to the bar. I knew he would be dead this time next week and I was pleased, really pleased. Does that sound harsh?
It was Friday – quiz night. Not my forte you may think. To be effective at quizzes you would think a memory would be a useful asset. So for a person who couldn't even remember the person who had sent him away for seven years you'd think this would be a disadvantage. Not so. I was good at puzzles. My specialised subject was golf, champions and championships. You'd think I would have forgotten all that with my memory loss but apparently not. I must be using a different part of my brain.
There was a noise and the Friends of Mynydd Eimon meeting finished. The anointed ones wandered amongst their adoring public. Cai pointed out the one who sat next to my sister.
"Dr Caddoc." He announced in a stage whisper, "Amos to his friends."
I remember quite a bit about the good doctor. He was taller now, balder and even more arrogant. I could tell this just by looking at him. The way he laughed, drank his beer? Held my sister around the waist. He was annoying me a little, even though I liked the guy.
I smiled and walked over the table. I nodded at my sister and asked Amos if I could talk to him.
"Make an appointment." He said, "You know how to make an appointment – just put your lips together and whistle." He thought it was hilarious. It wasn't.

I made an appointment in my head to see him the following day.

DAY 2

Standing in a clubhouse – not Mynydd Eimon. I'd won. Again. Exhilarated. Again. Exhilarated. Again and again and again. But this was the final time. I had the highs, the rush, the joy of being perfect. Now I was coming down like the junkie I was – cold turkey – Christmas - tired. So tired, golf, golf, golf. Guilty. I need to go. Need to leave. My damage here is done. Leave. Cut the cord – Gordian knot. Friends – used. Family – used. Loyal to nothing, no-one. It's just a game – I play. "I know you all" – golf as tedious as work – tired – bored. I get it. Now let me go. I'm a man now – 20, 1,2,3,4,5,6, ... let me go – please. Does it matter anyway? Who cares? St. Andrew? St. Andrews? A battered old goose-necked putter? I'm going home. You're not. Married. Tired. So tired. "Show me the way to go home."

8. out of the past

I woke up at 5 o'clock, as usual, with a blinding headache and a half-remembered dream.
 I had a feeling of loss and confusion from the dream. Nothing unusual there but in this particular dream I also had the sense of exhilaration, of winning. It tapped into some memory of myself as a success. I dressed, grabbed some golf clubs, some balls and wandered up to the golf course. I went into the unlocked clubhouse to the unlocked glass case with the putter. I opened the case and held the familiar putter. I slipped it in my bag and went out onto the course.
It was cold, misty and foggy. I could just make out the flag on the first green from the tee 400 yards or so away. I hit 2 smooth 5 irons to the green and holed a 6 feet putt for a birdie. The feeling of exhilaration evoked the same emotion as the dream, as I knew it would.
I walked around the course slowly and played as if back in the dream. I was 4 under when I reached the clubhouse again after the first 9 holes. I stopped and wandered back down the hill. It was all starting to come into focus now.
I ambled along Waterloo Road, smoking and thinking, thinking and smoking. I turned left onto Alma Road and my house. I went upstairs and changed then walked downstairs to the office. No sign of life anywhere.
I opened my desk and retrieved the report I had taken from the school. It was quite thin with sheets of numbers, natal charts and dates that I couldn't quite understand.
Most of the papers were boring – exam results, horary charts, yearly reports, etc. nothing at all interesting. All disappointing. I looked at my school file. There was one interesting sheet though. It was a summary of my school career;

Name: Samael Watcher
Born Sagittarius
Educated Mynydd Eimon
Family Details:
Father: Samael

Born: Ophiuchus;
Educated: Mynydd Eimon
Occupation Conflict consultant
Mother: Ishtar
Born Virgo;
Educated: Mynydd Eimon
Sibling: Seren
Born: Sagittarian;
Educated: Mynydd Eimon

Scholastic report

Attendance – absences : none unaccounted for
(see medical report Dr Caddoc)

Sports attainment

Captain rugby (Under 12, Under 13, Under 14)
Captain golf (Under 12, Under 13, Under 14)
Runner up Ystrad Cup 3 occasions

Summary Family report

Father away a great deal on business – good provider
Mother – disappeared
Guardian – Mary Lileth-Llad

Character report

aloof – intelligent – arrogant
(someone had scribbled 'killer' underneath)

This pretty much tied up with some of what my sister had told me. She had remembered a few things now. Or at least she had decided to tell me now.

According to my sister our father spent a lot of time on the road. Travelled around the world helping people, she thought. She said our uncle Daniel looked after things at home – money and so on. I believed her. I tried to remember something about Daniel. There was something about him I didn't like. I saw a lot of him when I was growing up, apparently. I had feelings rather than memories of distrust. I know my father was away a lot. No-one would tell me truthfully what he was doing. But I'm sure it was important. "Conflict resolution", my sister had called it. This seemed to be confirmed. I liked confirmation.

I have a vague memory of my father as a kind man, strong and stubborn. A bit like me I guess. Except he was more focused. Extremely focused. He wanted the best for me. "I'll do whatever it takes to make you the best ", he once told me. And he did – except he was never there when I needed him.

Golf. He loved golf with an intense passion. His ultimate dream was for me to be the best golfer in the world, "The next Bobby Jones ", he dreamed. I'd never heard of Bobby Jones but I was told that he was going to be the best golfer in the world. My father wanted me to be the best golfer in the world. And maths. Numbers. He had a thing about numbers. It was irrational I know, but he did seem to love numbers and his work. He felt that he was making a difference. "Fighting the good fight "I remember him saying. Actually, I seemed to be remembering a lot more about my father.

My mother I didn't seem to remember anything. I remember a vague memory of her as a star, a perfect vision of an angel. But I remember I was only three at the time.

My father never talked to my sister very much, so she claimed. I got the impression that my father didn't like women very much – not even my mother. I think it's a trait I seem to have adopted as well.

This was pretty much as my sister Seren had told me. I had some more confirmation now. I liked confirmation. I needed more though. I needed to check a few things. Well quite a few things. With quite a few people. My headache was coming back.

I was pretty much remembering now what my sister had told me. I felt comfortable with myself for the first time in a long time. I was filling in gaps. Getting completions. It felt good.

9: the interrupted journey

I waited a while for Lily to return to the office after lunch. I wanted to get the key to the safe. She didn't arrive. She was normally incredibly reliable. I began to worry. Not enough to contact her though. I needed to get out – needed to walk. Needed to see Doctor Caddoc, Amos to his friends. Practically my brother in law, apparently, according to Lily.
I turned left from the office, along Alma Road toward Lucknow Lane. I turned right onto Waterloo Road and walked into the large garden of Dr Caddoc's surgery. I went inside.
The waiting room had 17 people there. Caddoc's receptionist Rose (he had a receptionist, as I did) told me that Dr Caddoc was busy and refused to let him know I was there. We talked – I think I impressed her with my arguments. I said I would wait. I sat down and waited. 2 hours later I was the last man sitting.
I had plenty of time to look at the room. It was cold, clinical. Well, just a surgery would be – you would think. What struck me was that it was totally opposite to the Doctor. Caddoc was shambolic in every way, as I recall. Disorganised but charming in a funny sort of way. I tended to like him, for all his million faults.
The people in the surgery didn't look ill at all. There was deathly quiet – no coughs, no sneezes. Oh actually there was one person coughing. He coughed every 7 minutes. Exactly 7 minutes. I checked. The patients were buzzed in exactly on time. No-one looked at me – thank God.
Rose the receptionist coldly announced, "Mr Watcher, Dr Caddoc will see you now."
I stood up.
"He's in the room marked Dr Caddoc." She added unnecessarily.
I smiled like it didn't bother me and went along the corridor with pictures of lungs, cigarettes, babies and teeth. I knocked and waited for the word. It came immediately;
"Come".
The doctor's room was exactly like the waiting room – cold, white, new-looking.

Caddoc greeted me enthusiastically, almost as if he hadn't asked his receptionist to keep me waiting, "Sam. How's the dick work these days?"
"Quiet" I replied.
He giggled. "Don't lie to me, Sam. Sit, sit"
I sat sat.
"What can I do you for?" he asked
"Tell me the truth? " I asked expectantly.
"Never gonna happen. Too much. Too complicated. You don't need to
know." he enthused. He was a person who enthused about anything. Everything.
"OK. Tell me one thing then. "
"What do you *really* want to know?"
He took a cigarette from a packet, offered one to me. I nodded. He lit his own cigarette and mine and handed it to me. I took a long, long drag and thought.
"If we could start somewhere near the beginning that would be good"
He thought about it. He was the baby of the committee even though he wasn't the youngest. He had always been immature, fiery, hugely talented at golf and not too good at doctoring as I remember from some years ago. I heard him talking somewhere in the back of my head, so asked him to repeat it. Then I tuned back in.
"I said it was a number of years ago and you were ill. "
"What was wrong with me?"
"Oh some sort of illness." He took a long drag of his cigarette.
"?". I silently asked.
"You know. A disease sort of thing." Nice to see his doctoring skills had been well tuned over the missing years.
"You left 7 years ago," he announced as if it was the most amazing piece of knowledge in the world.
I sighed. "When? What month?"
"Oh Junish. Early summer – maybe July. I think."
He lit another cigarette from his almost finished cigarette, thought hard and continued, "No. It was May or June. After

Easter anyway. I remember because it was after the celebrations. Anyway we had to send you away."
"Where?"
"Oh somewhere far away. America I think"
"You think. Didn't you have to sign a medical report or form or something?"
"Probably. But it was a long time ago. I can't remember everything."
"Like me." I sighed
"Oh you will Sam. You will remember. Sometime"
"When?" I asked
"Tomorrow I guess."
I looked at him quizzically silently demanding more information. He heard me. "But I'm not sure what time tomorrow. I'm a doctor not a prophet."
"So you say. But to be blunt, you're not a very good doctor."
"Ah but I'm a terrible prophet" he roared with laughter as if it was hilarious.
It wasn't.
"I know I was Bobby Jones." I fished.
"You do?" He stopped laughing.
"Yes."
"Ah, so you already know you went to America in 1923?"
"Of course." I lied. I had a thought, "So what year is it now then?" I asked.
Dr Caddoc waved the question away and continued,
"We had to get you to Atlanta 1923. It was tricky I can tell you."
"Who are 'we'?"
"All of us of course. And anyway it was tricky. Then bringing you back was trickier." He thought for a while then decided he would tell the truth, "Not that I had anything to do with it mind. I'm not really the one they turn to for anything technical. "
"Or medical." I volunteered.
"Or medical," he repeated and roared with laughter.
"So how did it work?" I continued.
"Magik." (pause). "Anything else I can help you with?"
"Did my father suggest it?"

The doctor looked at me blankly with a slight smile. He continued, "Anything else?"

"Today's date?"

"Not relevant"

Realising I was on a roll now I asked, "Tell me more"

"No. No. No."

"You've said too much?" I asked

"Oh no. I've said exactly the right amount".

He grinned a shit-eating grin.

We shook hands like grown-ups are supposed to do. We both looked a little uncomfortable. He was grinning as if he had won some sort of a prize. I left and walked along Waterloo Road until I reached the old ruins. I strode purposefully on the stones. I was very confused now. I decided I needed a sidekick. I needed someone to talk to – a literary device to discuss my ideas with – but that would come later with the stage version, wireless series and eventually the film of the book. For now I had to be satisfied with me and my own head.

"Perhaps it could be a woman, some love interest. " I said to myself.

"I shouldn't think so. "I replied "That would be too complicated, and out of character."

 "Stop thinking about this now. " I voiced, "We've got a case to crack."

"Right." I thought. I also thought that if I could solve what had happened to me I would solve the incredible case of the murder that hadn't happened yet. I reasoned that it was too much of a coincidence that Mynydd Eimon would have two interesting and separate events going on simultaneously. And anyway all story tellers know that coincidences to get characters into trouble are great; coincidences to get them out of it is cheating. So I decided to go home and examine the first set of documents I had been allowed to steal.

10. don't bother to knock

I went back to my office and found a sheet of paper on the desk. I guess it was from the folder and Lily had left it out for me. I deduced this from her note; *'Sheet from folder I thought you may like to see – Lily'*

Transvaal, South Africa 1895;
Shengting province, China 1899;
Chihuahua, Mexico 1910;
Sarejavo, Bosnia 1914;
Petrograde, Russia 1917;
Dublin 1922;
New York 1923;
Philadelphia 1924;
Columbus Ohio 1926;
Liverpool 1930;
Philadelphia 1930.

Why had Lily left me this list? I guess she was tired of waiting for me to find this in the folder so had given me a push. I would have found it eventually. Lily was getting a trifle impatient with my apparent lack of progress, I guess.
I left the house and went to the office of Daniel Llewellyn, family solicitor. He. Don. Il Corlione. Maybe not the Don. More like the Robert Duvall character. I turned left from Alma Road on to Maffeking Terrace. I then crossed Inkerman Street to Aliwar Avenue where I found the office. I knocked and went into the reception area – no secretary. It was a good office. Big. Lush. Plush. Better than mine – I reluctantly admitted to myself. But no secretary. I smiled.
I knocked on the inner door.
"Enter"
I opened a heavy oak door and walked into the office.
"Samael. Don't bother to knock. You're family. Come in."
I opened the heavy oak door and walked into the office.
Llewellyn was sat behind a huge oak table pretending to read

some important looking papers as if he didn't know I was coming to visit.

"Mr Llewellyn," I said.

He rose from his chair. As he rose the flabby fat around his middle jostled and wriggled underneath his expensive suit. His small piggy eyes narrowed as he smiled too easily, too sincerely. His voice was a throaty purr;

"Sam. Sam. Long-time no see". He waddled around the enormous desk and shook my hand warmly with both his hands. "And what's with this Mr Llewellyn nonsense. You're my favourite nephew."

I sat quietly, somewhat sheepishly. I've didn't like solicitors. Well, I didn't like this one.

"It doesn't seem appropriate to call you Uncle Daniel in your office." I explained.

He ignored me and thundered on.

"So Sam how have you been?" he asked even more warmly.

"Perhaps you could tell me"

"Oh Sam, always the joker "

"Or perhaps 'where' would be a more appropriate question"

"All in good time Sam. All in good time. "

He paused and looked carefully at me. He took out a cigar and slowly lit it.

"Didn't you want to talk about Mary's murder?" he continued, eventually.

"All in good time Daniel. All in good time." I said.

He smiled – slightly forced, but he disguised his annoyance well. "I can see traces of your father in you. I really can. But seriously, first things first. I hear you're working on a murder case. Mary?"

"Perhaps? How does it involve you?"

"Oh I'm involved Sam. I'm involved in everything."

"You've got details of the will, I guess?"

"Oh very good Sam. What else did you deduce?"

I waited for him to continue. He did.

"I assume you want to know how much you will be left."

"Not really. I'm not sure Cai has very much he can leave. He's a poor

Golf club professional, drinks a little, gambles a lot, lives in a room at the golf club. I'm pretty sure he's not likely to leave me millions."

"Correct. But he may leave you something even better. " Daniel continued

"Oh" I was genuinely surprised.

"His job Sam. His job"

"Golf professional?"

"With all that comes with it. All the benefits."

"Not interested Mr Llewellyn, I've already got a job"

"But this would be a real job." He looked hard at me and said, "You would have killed for this job a few years ago."

"Inappropriate. "

"Sorry. I'm sorry. But really Sam. Think about it. You could still play at Taff Noir or whatever you call. " he laughed loudly at his incredible wit.

I thought about it for twenty seconds thinking, "Golf Noir", then changed the subject.

"So when do we talk about my lost past?"

"We have an eternity for that. We need to talk about your current situation."

"No thanks. Client confidentiality and all that. "

"Really?" He looked genuinely surprised. It was clear he wasn't used to hearing the word 'no'. He waited 15 seconds then stood up to signify my time was up. In a moment of inspiration I realised why he had reacted as he had. He was afraid of me. I refused to move.

"Tell me about my father" I asked politely.

"Not now Sam. I'm busy". He wasn't.

"Tell me or I will tell him you ignored me" I used the threat of the schoolyard.

"Why is he known as Sam Draig?" I continued.

"Ysbryd Draig. To be absolutely correct," he tersely answered, "Because he's a ghost and a dragon. He's Welsh and proud. He used to be a fighter you know. "

"Used to be" I interrupted.

"He gave it up"

"Because he lost?" I asked

"No. Because he won." Came the reply.
"More enigmatic crap." I thought.
I asked about Chihuaha, Transvaal. Like me he thought they were not very nice places for holidays. I asked what business my father might have had at the start of a war, or a number of wars. He told me that my father used to help out. I didn't really see my father as a person who helped people out. I wondered what business reasons he could have for being at the start of the Russian revolution, Mexican revolution, etcetera. Daniel repeated that he was helping out. I didn't like to think of my father as an arms dealer but there seemed few other options unless he was a peace maker. A pretty terrible peace maker by the looks of it given his 100 percent failure rate.
He even shed some light on family history I had forgotten. He told me about my father in a fair amount of detail. Apparently in the early years my father was a bit of a wanderer. He never stayed in one place long. Then he'd arrived in Wales with Daniel, Amos, Cai and a few friends and stayed. He'd fallen in love with my mother and had his wings clipped for a few years. When myself and my sister were born he went back to his old ways. I waited for more.
"Sam. That's enough." He said with a sense that it was all I was going to get, "Your father will tell you the rest when he returns. "
"When will that be?" I asked.
"*No-one knows the day or hour.*" Daniel began waxing lyrical, "*not even the angels in heaven, but he will come like a thief in the night*"
I looked quizzically at him.
He laughed. "Just joking Sam, Just joking. I really have no idea where he is now. China, maybe? "
Finally he succeeded in moving me to the door. I found myself looked at an oak door I was out of the office looking at the plush, lush reception area.
I had a headache.
I went back to my office – saw my secretary for a few minutes and got the key to the safe. I asked a few questions about Cai, my sister and my parents. She told me a few more lies.
I ate. I wept. I felt tired. So tired.

11: open secret

I fell asleep at my desk and woke up late in the afternoon. I woke up with a blinding headache.
I opened the bottom drawer of my desk and pulled out some headache tablets. I swallowed them with a glass of water. As I finished drinking I noticed the key that had appeared in my desk drawer. Lily must have anticipated that I would need it. She did that a lot. I must remember to give her a raise when I start paying her.
I made myself a cup of coffee. I unlocked the safe with the key, took out the folder I had taken from the golf club and laid it carefully on my desk.
I sorted the contents of the folder into golf cuttings, accounts, bible references, random snippets, pictures, and an etcetera pile. There weren't too many documents. Mostly they were invoices and accounts for the golf club and business trips for my father and Cai's father, Michael.
It seemed that the lack of effort collect golf fees from Aunty Mary was channelled into her accounting process. Mynydd Eimon golf club HR department seemed to consist solely of aunty Mary. It was her handwriting on the accounts, her documenting and numbering the various invoices, train, bus and air tickets.
The main sheet consisted of the list of places I had been given by Lily. That was supplemented with cross-references invoices, tickets, receipts.
There was a handwritten page that looked incredibly old. As I read it I noticed it was not written in an olde fashionede stylee;

The Story of Golf – 1. Andrew on the Beach at Patras
"So, what was he like then, as a boss?"
"Good. A bit quiet, but really good to work for."
"In what way?"
"Well. He just left you alone to get on with really. Trust. He trusted you totally. What more would you want in a leader?"
"Nothing...sounds good. You were the first weren't you?"
"I was. Well at least alphabetically I was", he laughed
"..... and now the last." he sighed.

It had been a hard ten years but now it was nearly over. They had spent a month in Patras and their journey was coming to an end. The pair walked further along the seafront towards something lying on the sand. Andrew bent down to pick up a longish, thinnish piece of driftwood and started examining it, "Gopher Wood." he announced.
"Wasn't that the wood from the ark?"
"It was," announced Andrew as he started swinging it. Maximilla found some circular pebbles and before long the child-like pair were hitting the pebbles along the deserted beach.
As they rounded the cove they saw a crowd of soldiers marching toward them. They stood still as Aegeas and twenty one soldiers rushed forward and grabbed Andrew. The soldiers began dragging him away toward a small group of soldiers holding a decussate cross on the sand. He leaned over to Maximilla and resigned to his fate, whispered, "Remember these last moments."

In the folder there were a number of clippings of golfer Bobby Jones clipped together chronologically from July 16th 1923 to July 2nd 1930. Each delicately clipped clipping was from a range of newspapers from either America or Britain, Some regional, some national;

'CROWDS HAIL JONES ON RETURN TO U.S. 'from the Memphis Evening Appeal;

'BOBBY JONES WINS IN OPEN' from the Daily Express;

'JONES WINS BIG GOLF TITLE FOR FOURTH IN ROW' from the Bethlehem Globe-Times;

'GRAND SLAM JONES.' from somewhere else.

There were pages and pages of them clipped together with a huge bulldog clip. I read each one. I had a sense of seeing these events myself somehow or dreaming them.
There were pictures of Bobby Jones;

Bobby Jones' holding his battered old goose-necked putter that seemed incredibly familiar,
A picture of Bobby Jones on his wedding day with 'childhood sweetheart Mary Rice Malone';
Bobby Jones in a variety of golfing poses;
A photograph of 2 children playing with a sculpture of Bobby Jones. On the back was written 'Clara and Bobby';
Bobby Jones at Augusta;
Bobby Jones at Merion;
Bobby Jones at St Andrews;
Bobby Jones at Hoylake.

There were a lot of Bobby Jones pictures and newspaper cuttings. As I looked through them I started crying. By the time I'd finished I was gripping the pictures tightly and sobbing uncontrollably. This was quite unusual for me.
Eventually I stopped and carefully put them back in the folder. There was a copy of the list Lily had left for me. The dates corresponded to wars or golf tournaments. I guessed it was tied

in to my father's consultancy service and his love of golf. Maybe. Maybe.

There were clips and articles about Bobby Jones, by various hands.

One in particular was interesting. It was a page cut out of a golf magazine;

> He was only twenty-eight years old and Bobby Jones announced his retirement from all golfing competition. The greatest golfer the world had ever known had played in his last championship. He had finished off the seven fat years with thirteen major championships. In the closing year 1930, he had accomplished the impossible - winning all four major titles.
> I recalled an incident in an upstairs room at the Interlachen Club a few months earlier. I put my hand on his shoulder and asked him: "Bobby, when are you going to quit this darned game?"
> Bobby looked a shade more serious. "I don't know," he said, "but pretty soon, I think. I am awfully tired."

There were invoices and a ledger of accounts. Train tickets, air tickets, hotel rooms. Seems the Friends of Mynydd Eimon were very organised financially. I looked at some of the entries - they tended to agree with the list I had seen. There were invoices for guns, bullets and meals.

The final entry, unlike most of the others was not in Aunty Mary's ornate writing, but scrawled in barely legible red ink. Or something that looked like red ink. It was a list of names;

Samyaza L. Watcher
Daniel Llewellyn
Pedr Penn
Barry Abloec
Amos Caddoc
Mary Lileth-Llad
~~Cai Tywysog~~   Samael Watcher

I tried to work out if this was good or bad news.
I sat and thought. Thought and smoked. For maybe an hour.

12: angel face

I left the office. It was cold and I didn't have a hat, a gun anything, I had barely remembered my coat. I was tired, upset and fed up of feeling manipulated. I knew I was being crowded, manipulated and laughed at. I hurried, head down along Alma Street, turned left onto Balaclava Road then left into Taganarog Terrace walking quicker all the time. By the time I reached my sister's house I was practically running. The door was open. I walked into the front room. It felt warm and it felt cosy. The room was void of Dr, Caddoc, which was a relief. It was messy however and the chairs weren't in their proper assigned places. The table wasn't pushed properly back against the wall. There was a mirror on the wall that wasn't quite straight. It was clean but not tidy. Stressful.

There was something else out of place, my sister. She was sitting on the floor. She had been crying. She was looking at a photo of our mother. I had never seen the photo before. It was a snap of me, my sister and mother on a beach somewhere. We looked happy. We looked warm. My sister looked up at me as I moved around the room. Her eyes were red, really red.

"Sit down" she said, "You're making the place look untidy."

It was a joke. I didn't laugh.

I sat on the settee near her and looked at the photo.

"This was taken the week before you left."

I froze inwardly.

I had been thinking a lot the past hour and finally realised how much I was being manipulated. I had come to my sister's to see if there was one person in the whole village who wasn't controlling me – there obviously wasn't.

My sister looked up to me. Her face indicated that she had taken my facial expression as a sign of an outpouring of grief for our poor departed mother.

"What happened to her?" I decided to play along with the charade. I didn't have a better plan.

"I don't know – she disappeared a few days later."

She wiped away a tear. Then she looked at me to see if it was working. I wasn't going to cry if I could help it. I did look sad though as I suddenly realised that she must have blamed me for our mothers' disappearance.

As my sister acted out her lines it confirmed a number of things I had remembered. Our parents had argued a lot over the years because of his work. Apparently he wasn't the easiest man to live with. He had a short temper, an obnoxious attitude and was inclined to be selfish. I had heard it all before from my mother.

"Tell me something I don't know about our mother." I asked.

"She was kind, gentle."

"That's not what I remember"

"She was"

"Really?"

She looked at me, reconsidered and slowly replied;

"No. She was tough and pretty. She looked like Ingrid Bergman. She wasn't gentle though. She fought to keep you here."

She handed me the photo. I looked carefully at it. She did look like Ingrid Bergman in the film Casablanca that I must have seen sometime. She had the face of an angel, ironically. My mother not Ingrid Bergman. Well, both really.

Seren continued; "Our mum loved you. So much. She loved you more than anyone in this world. She couldn't bear the thought of you turning into your father. She tried to stop it but our fathers mind was set. She knew you were going away and that when you returned you would not be the boy you once were".

I was impressed with the scriptwriter, whoever it was.

"And...." I prompted.

"And you went away"

"Why?"

We both knew why I had to go away. I had to leave. Complete my education, my initiation. To make me ready.

She didn't need to speak.

"And mum?"

"She went away. She didn't want you following him, didn't want you to be like him. He decreed that you would go into the family business. She didn't want it. So she went away".

"Where is she?"

She looked at me as if I were an idiot. She became genuinely tearful. Finally she went off message.

"She's dead obviously. He killed her."
"But you don't just kill someone because of a disagreement."
"When else would you kill someone?"
"You know what I mean"
Then more quietly she said, "You killed her."
"And you hate me."
She looked at me again as if I were an idiot.
"What about the police?"
This was the third time she looked at me as if I were a total idiot.
Silence.
I decided to try as hard as I could not to ask any more questions.
She decided to clarify, for the record, exactly what an idiot I was; "What about the police? Oh come on. This is Mynydd Eimon. This is Wales, I've never seen a policeman. Have you? Doesn't that seem strange to you?"
I had to ask one more question; "Will I remember her?"
"Soon. Tomorrow. On your birthday."
"It's not my birthday."
"It is. It's a surprise."
I couldn't stop myself, "But why are you telling me this now?"
"Because it's important – he's coming for you soon."
Silence.
I didn't bother to say anything. Then decided to try something; "Look sis. We were close once. But it was a long time ago. I've changed. You've changed. Me, you and our parents. Sure we had problems, but it doesn't take much to see that the problems of four people don't amount to a hill of beans in this crazy world. Someday you'll understand that. "
My sister lowered her head and began to cry.
"Sorry. Thought it would cheer you up."
I sat down. I poured myself a bourbon straight up. I sighed. It looked like she was going to cry again. I didn't have time for this. I had a case to solve. My filial relationship problems could be sorted later.
I finished my drink and left, barely looking at my sister. I didn't hate her for anything – how could I? She hadn't done anything wrong – probably. But I looked at her and couldn't remember her. I knew she hated me. I knew she had been used to

manipulate me by someone. Judging by the speech, probably my old headmaster. I left.

I walked the streets feeling the warmth of the drink fighting the cold of the fog. It was going to be a long night.

I needed a priest

13. angels with dirty faces

"Barry. Tell me about the bible."
"Ah, which bit?"
"The Book of Enoch "
I watched as Father Barry smiled. We were in the church. In the aisle. He was happy. He was enthused and thrilled about something. He still looked like a tramp however.
"Then said the Most High, the Holy and Great One spake, and sent Uriel to the son of Lamech, and said to him: 'Go to Noah and tell him in my name "Hide thyself!" and reveal to him the end that is approaching: that the whole earth will be destroyed, and a deluge is about to come upon the whole earth, and will destroy all that is on it." He recited
"No. before that."
"Ah but this is relevant. This is the beginning, or part of the beginning."
I had had enough of this enigmatic nonsense. I decided to express myself assertively. I reached out and coolly grabbed Barry by the throat and whispered; "Barry. Just fucking tell me"
He tried to get away and blustered in a cartoon way. I let him go and he shook himself like a dog.
"Just like your father", he announced as his smoothed his collar. He calmed himself and continued.
"It's part of the story. The ark, salvation, gopher wood, golf, St. Andrew, St Andrews. You've got nearly all the pieces now Sam. You're good at puzzles aren't you?"
"I thought I was. "
"It's all there; *And it came to pass when the children of men had multiplied that in those days were born unto them beautiful and comely daughters. And the angels, the children of the heaven, saw and lusted after them, and said to one another: "*
I finished the reading for Barry, "*'Come, let us choose us wives from among the children of men and beget us children."*
 "Yes. You are one of the begotten." he announced triumphantly and redundantly.

I was bored. I looked up at Barry. He was no help. I started to walk away. Father Barry chased after me – desperate. I realise he was terrified of me for some reason.

"Sam – you know the truth already. You just don't want to accept it. Accept it."

I stopped and turned.

"Tell me about angels?"

"What?"

"What do they look like Barry? Do they have wings?"

He laughed, "No Sam. We don't have wings. We look as normal as you and I," he paused, "Or your father or Amos or Daniel or Cai. We have to travel by train. We're not Spidermen or demons. We can't read minds or kill people with a single thought or leap tall buildings. "He considered some of the better points; "We can mess with time - bring bits of the future forward. Anticipate. We can be quite manipulative."

"Really?"

"So what happened with my father and Cai's father?"

"Ah Michael"

He recited;

"Samael took hold of the wings of Michael whom he wished to bring down with him in his fall; but Michael was saved by God. "He paused.

"However that's not strictly true." He explained.

"How do you know?"

"I was there. Or at least this was how it appeared to me in a vision when I wrote it. But I made up the last bit."

"About God saving him?

Yes. So what really happened then?"

"They had a fight and he fell off a cliff. "

"Really. The angels had a fight?"

"Of course. Sort of. Sam landed on Michael who was killed. It was an accident."

I went home and slept. My head felt as if it would explode.

DAY 3

I could see. The bandages came off my eyes and I could see – Augusta – family – Mary – Clara – golf - I liked golf – not because of the love of the game – but to please my father – pathetic. I saw parts of it connect – a story line – Noah - gopher wood – the battered old goose-necked putter - St Andrew –St Andrews - good – bad - yin – yan - black – white - richer for poorer - son and daughters - Cai and Sam - Sam and Michael - Spade and Archer. Behold, I am coming soon, bringing my recompense with me, to repay everyone for what he has done. Hallelujah free at last -

14. stolen face

I awoke.
It was a bright shiny Sag day. November 30th.
I had been used. That was then. This was now.
My headache was gone and so were my visions – my full Old Testament revelations - Real Father Barry visions - Maybe revelations rather than visions - Maybe memories as well as revelations.
I had been used. That was then. This was now.
Memories came back to me. I remembered my mother. I remembered my seven years in Atlanta. I remembered my family, my wife, children, parents, smiles, tears. All gone. I remembered I had no family now. No wife. No children. Borrowed then stolen. All gone. Some never existed. My fathers' words, "You need to learn about life. About people, ordinary people. Find out what makes them tick. Get married. Have a family. Seek wisdom. "
I remembered everything. I did hate Cai, Barry and Daniel.
I got ready for the golf tournament with Cai. Fuck.
I had been used. I was still being used.

15. the killing

"Aunty Mary! Aunty Mary!" he called as he pushed open the front door and walked along the passageway. He looked into the front room on his right at the perfectly clean armchairs and sofa and once again cursed himself for wasting 5 seconds of his life looking for Mary in a room that was never used except for Sundays, or for visitors – or the police. He closed the door quietly and listened.
He heard a noise from upstairs as Mary Ap Gwelym shuffled across the bedroom toward the stairs. He walked back through the passageway to the foot of the stairs, "Aunty Mary. Come down now. I've got something to tell you.....some news."
She left her duster on the dressing table and moved gingerly down the stairs.
"Old age doesn't come by itself." she muttered to herself.
Slowly, slowly she descended, tentatively placing her foot on the mat at the foot of the stairs and closed the open front door.
"What's all this palaver cariad?" she asked
"I just came to tell you about the Ystrad Cup. I was second. I know I usually win but Sam won it. He played really well. I'm so pleased for him. So glad he's back... A bit of a surprise that?" he beamed.
Mary seemed genuinely surprised and hobbled into the front room.
"Well that wasn't in the script", she announced.
He followed her into the room, "No-one expected it. Great isn't it?"
"Diaown" answered Mary. She opened the drawer of the Welsh dresser, reached in, pulled an army revolver and fired 3 shots into his heart.

16. thirteenth hour

Later.

I went into the garden. I saw my father in the garden. He was standing under an elm tree smoking – half turned away from me – unaware. He did look like Nosferatu. He really did, which was strange in that he wasn't that skinny, but he had long, skinny fingers holding a long, skinny cigarette. It must have been that which accentuated it. He seemed to have evil seeping from every pore. He turned to me…..
Honestly…….he looked incredibly normal. He had a dark suit and a small goatee with accentuated the smallness of his mouth. He turned and saw me and moved, almost glided, he did – he almost glided, toward me. I had no idea how old he was. How did age work with angels? He looked about 40ish. His last few steps toward me were slower, almost warily.
His face said sorry before his mouth did. I had no idea what to do. So I asked the question;
"What about my mother?" I asked
"Human" was the reply
"Me?"
"Who knows? Never happened before. Maybe you'll take after me and maybe live forever or maybe your mother……" He stopped
"Tell me about my mother?"
"No, she's gone."
I waited
"I loved her. I give up Heaven for her. Well it wasn't that much of a sacrifice I was fed up anyway. I needed space. Needed to move. Branch out of my own. Move somewhere better"
"Wales?"
"Why not? If we had picked somewhere like Etheopia, Persia, Turkey it would have been better?"
He smiled.
I didn't.
"Cai and Michael?" I asked.

"Michael was a good friend. He was on our side once. A long time ago. Cai was weak."
I didn't hug him. I didn't say "Oh father forgive me for I have forsaken you." or anything. I just walked past him and went along Aliwar Avenue, Inkerman Street and Ladysmith Road to the old ruins.
All the time I walked I recited a story we had had to learn in Sunday school;
"And there was war in heaven: Michael and his angels fought against the dragon; and the dragon fought and his angels, And prevailed not; neither was their place found any more in heaven. And the great dragon was cast out, that old serpent, called the Devil, and Satan, which deceiveth the whole world: he was cast out into the earth, and his angels were cast out with him. "

Made in the USA
Charleston, SC
15 April 2014